The Entertainer

and the
Dybbuk

SID FLEISCHMAN

The Entertainer

and the
Dybbuk

Greenwillow Books
An Imprint of HarperCollins*Publishers*

ALSO BY SID FLEISCHMAN

The Whipping Boy

The Scarebird

The Ghost in the Noonday Sun

The Midnight Horse

McBroom's Wonderful One-Acre Farm

Here Comes McBroom!

Mr. Mysterious & Company

Chancy and the Grand Rascal

The Ghost on Saturday Night

Jim Ugly

The 13th Floor

The Abracadabra Kid

Bandit's Moon

A Carnival of Animals

Bo and Mzzz Mad

Disappearing Act

The Giant Rat of Sumatra

Escape! The Story of The Great Houdini

The White Elephant

For the million and a half

The Entertainer and the Dybbuk
Copyright © 2008 by Sid Fleischman

The text of this book is set in 12-point Aldine 401.
Book design by Sylvie Le Floc'h.

Library of Congress Cataloging-in-Publication Data
Fleischman, Sid, (date).
The entertainer and the dybbuk / Sid Fleischman.
   p. cm.
"Greenwillow Books."
Summary: A struggling American ventriloquist in post-World War II Europe is possessed by the mischievous spirit of a young Jewish boy killed in the Holocaust. Author's note details the murder of over one million children by the Nazis during the 1930s and 1940s.
ISBN-13: 978-0-06-134445-9 (trade bdg.) ISBN-10: 0-06-134445-1 (trade bdg.)
ISBN-13: 978-0-06-134446-6 (lib. bdg.) ISBN-10: 0-06-134446-X (lib. bdg.)
Holocaust, Jewish (1939-1945)—Juvenile fiction.
[1. Holocaust, Jewish (1939-1945)—Fiction. 2. Jews—Europe—Fiction.
3. Dybbuk—Fiction. 4. Spirit possession—Fiction. 5. Ghosts—Fiction.
6. Ventriloquism—Fiction.] I. Title.
PZ7.F5992En 2007 [Fic]—dc22 2007017267

First Edition 10 9 8 7 6 5 4 3 2 1

 Greenwillow Books

The decision had to be made to annihilate . . . every Jewish child and to make this people disappear from the face of the earth. This is being accomplished.

—Heinrich Himmler, chief hangman of the Nazi Holocaust, and leader of the dreaded German SS squads, in a 1943 speech. Strutting about like vultures in black uniforms, SS killers wore death-skull insignias on their caps.

The Entertainer

and the
Dybbuk

CHAPTER

➤ 1 ⬥

In the gray, bombed-out city of Vienna, Austria, an American ventriloquist opened the closet door of his hotel. Still in his tuxedo and overcoat, The Great Freddie intended to put away the battered suitcase in which he carried his silent wooden dummy. But there on the floor sat a gaunt man with arms folded across his knees, waiting. After a second glance,

The Great Freddie realized it was a child, a long-legged child with the hungry look of a street kid. In the deep shadows the intruder glowed faintly, as if sprayed with moonlight.

"Well, well, howdy," said the ventriloquist, startled. "Waiting for a bus?"

"Waiting for you, Mr. Yankee Doodle, sir."

The entertainer, thin as a cornstalk from his native Nebraska, grinned and shucked his overcoat. Someone's idea of a prank, was this? "If you're under the notion that all Yanks are millionaires and an easy touch, you may go through my pockets. I'm just about broke. Tapped out. Down to bedrock."

"*Feh!* Who needs your money?" asked the intruder. "I once saved your life."

"You don't say."

"Would I lie to you?"

"You're a mouthy kid," the lanky American remarked. "I've never laid eyes on you."

"Want to bet, Sergeant?"

Sergeant? The Great Freddie's cat-green eyes narrowed as he peered into the closet. Confound this pest. How had he known that Freddie T. Birch, second-rate ventriloquist, had been in uniform? The big war in Europe had ended three years before. It was now 1948. Freddie's army haircut had long ago grown out. Now in his early twenties, he parted his hair in the middle and slicked it back, shiny as glass. What had tipped off this kid?

"Lucky guess," the entertainer said

finally. What was it with the boy's eyes? They were unnaturally bright, as if lit from within. "Who are you, a kid actor from one of the theaters? I know makeup when I see it. You're painted up white as Caesar's ghost."

"I am a ghost," replied the intruder.

"Don't make me laugh."

"Am I cracking jokes, Mr. Yank?"

The Great Freddie, growing impatient, wanted to brush his teeth and tumble into bed. "Go haunt someone else. I can see your sharp elbows. Ghosts are wisps of fog."

"Sorry to disappoint you," said the intruder.

"Anyway, pal, I've never heard of a ghost in short pants."

"Excuse me, there are lots of us. Did they keep it a secret from you in the army? The Holocaust? Adolf Hitler—may he choke forever on herring bones! You didn't hear he told his Nazi *meshuggeners*, those lunatics, 'Soldiers of Germany, have some fun and go murder a million and a half Jewish kids? All ages! Babies, fine. Girls with ribbons in their hair, why not? Boys in short pants, like Avrom Amos Poliakov? That's me, and how do you do? No, I wasn't old enough for long pants. Me, not yet a bar mitzvah boy when the long-nosed German SS officer shot me and left me in the street to bleed to death. So, behold, you see a dybbuk in short pants, not yet thirteen but older'n God."

The Great Freddie took a deep breath. He was dimly aware that Hitler, the sputtering dictator with the fungus of a mustache, had sent children to his slaughterhouses. But so many?

Ugly vote by vote, the Germans had elected a lunatic to run their country. Freddie wasted no pity on the once-proud survivors who had voted him into power. They had drowned democracy like a kitten, invaded Poland and France and ignited World War II. Now Germany lay bombed into a rubble of fallen roofs and shattered lives. Freddie had volunteered to do his part.

The former bombardier cleared his mind of the war. "So you're a ghost in short pants."

"A dybbuk."

"A what?"

"I said, a dybbuk. A spirit. With tsuris. That means trouble in my native language, Mr. Far-Away America. Think of me as a Jewish imp. I need to possess someone's body for a while, rent free. You're kind of tall and skinny, but I won't complain."

The ventriloquist cocked an eye. "Has anyone told you you're a sassy kid or dybbuk or whatever you are?"

"When you dodge Nazi soldiers for years, why not? When you hide in sewers and then knock around with dybbuks for more years, your tongue sharpens like an ice pick. You'd prefer baby talk?"

"I'd prefer you attach yourself to some-one else," said the ventriloquist. "I've got no time for a snotty spirit hanging on to me like a leech. I have enough trouble of my own."

"And no wonder, Mr. Entertainer," said the dybbuk. "I caught your act. You move your lips like a carp."

"And I'll bet you snuck in the theater."

"Why not?" replied the dybbuk. "Don't I come from a family of actors?"

The ventriloquist wondered if the glass of dinner wine he'd had after his last perform-ance had gone to his head. "Why am I talking to you?" he asked aloud. "I don't believe in ghosts."

"You want to know the truth," replied the dybbuk, "neither do I. But here I am, fit as a fiddle."

The Great Freddie kicked the closet door shut. He was hallucinating, wasn't he? Dreaming on his feet?

The ventriloquist pulled off his jacket and patent-leather shoes. Early the next morning he had a train to catch. He had been booked for a week across the border in Italy. He brushed his teeth, checked the sheets for postwar bedbugs, and fell into bed.

"Sleep tight," said the dybbuk through the closet door.

CHAPTER

❖ 2 ❖

On the train ride south, Freddie gazed out the window at the ruins of Europe. Like stage sets, buildings stood wide open with their fronts fallen away. The Italian train stations, one after the other, had been blown apart by pinpoint bombings. He had been one of the young Americans flying overhead to scatter the enemy's troops. He'd gotten a medal. Several.

Once the war was over, Freddie never wanted to fly again. He didn't even like to go up in elevators.

The woodsy town of Balzano appeared to be hiding in the Italian forest. Chilly clouds drifted through the treetops, and Freddie was glad he'd hung on to his old air corps flight jacket.

He was almost late for the theater. The orchestra below the stage—a piano, a fiddle, and a set of drums—thumped up a few bars of walk-on music. The Great Freddie grabbed his wooden puppet, strode onto the stage, and peered past the spotlight. Where was the audience?

He gripped the head stick and gave the dummy a quick look over the spotlights. *"Buona sera.* Anyone out there?"

He'd carved the comic face in a prisoner-of-war camp in Poland. Once the war was over, he'd stayed in Europe. He had no one to welcome him back home in Custer County, Nebraska. One-eighth Cherokee Indian, he had grown up an orphan.

He was still an orphan. It puzzled him to be the one, the only one of the crew, to walk away from the crash of his B-52 over the oil fields of Romania. He had known when joining up that he was cannon fodder. Someone was supposed to die in a war. Those were the rules. But now here he was, indisputably alive. What kind of cosmic joke was that? Why had he been spared? To make a hunk of pinewood talk?

Smiling in the spotlight, he gave the dummy's evening clothes a brush of his fingertips and straightened the flowing cape lined in bright red silk. He looked the puppet in the eye. "Is it true that you've decided to become a vampire and bite people on the neck?" he asked.

"Yup. Call me Count Dracula," replied the dummy.

"Vampires have a bad reputation."

"You should talk. Have you seen your act?"

"Vampires fly a lot," said the ventriloquist.

"Have you learned how to flap your wings like a bat?"

"Not me. I want to go somewhere, I call a taxi. Anyway, I'm afraid of heights."

"So am I."

"Look how tall you are. Maybe if you took a bath, you'd shrink."

"That's stupid, even for a block of wood."

"What do you expect, Einstein?"

Were they all dead out front? Freddie wondered.

"Hey, don't hold me so high. If I get airsick and throw up, will you know what to do?"

"What?"

"Duck."

The Great Freddie pulled a lever that opened the dummy's mouth wide, and he made barfing sounds.

At last, a meager laugh. Again looking past the spotlight, The Great Freddie thought he'd improve the act if he could throw his voice into the audience and shout "Bravo!"

"What did you do in the war, Count Dracula?"

"I volunteered."

"Volunteered for what?"

"The blood bank."

Freddie was pleased to detect a ripple of laughter. Blood bank. That was hard to say without touching your lips together. But as long as the count's mouth kept moving up and down, the illusion was perfect: The Great Freddie's voice seemed to come from the dummy.

Soon, a man leaning his chin on an umbrella handle began to heckle him. "Hey, Chicago! You're not supposed to move your lips!"

"Neither are you," Freddie retorted across the footlights. "And I'm not from Chicago."

He faced the dummy again, eye to eye. "Blood bank, did you say? That's gross, Count. I don't believe vampires really bite people on the neck to drink their blood."

"No?"

With his hand inside the dummy's clothing, Freddie whipped the count against his neck for a bite. He quickly reared back and away from the dummy's bite.

"Don't try that again!" Freddie warned.

"Why not?"

"I'll bite you back."

"You'll get splinters!"

The heckler was back. "I could see your lips move! Like a steam shovel!"

Freddie was barely able to hold his amiable smile. He'd learned his act in five languages, allowing him to gypsy around Europe. But wise guys came in ten languages. Freddie tried to ignore the pest.

"Do you vampires have any fun?" he asked the count.

"Sure. I get to see the world."

"What would you like to visit?"

"The Dead Sea. Ha! Ha!"

Once again, the dummy went for Freddie's throat. Yelled the ventriloquist, "I told you! Don't try biting me again!"

"Why not?"

"Haven't you noticed? You've got no teeth."

"Gott in Himmel!"

Said Freddie, "I didn't know you speak German."

"Professor, I never know what's coming out of your mouth."

The audience sat on its hands.

"Wake me when this is over!" the heckler called out.

Freddie fixed a scowl on the man. "Write this down. The bigger the mouth, the better it looks shut."

"Yeah," the count said, adding his two cents. "Who pulls your strings?"

Well, that'll get me fired, Freddie told himself.

He snuck out of the theater before the stage manager could collar him. In his hotel room, hardly larger than a birdcage, he opened the wicker suitcase to put a black blindfold over his dummy's eyes for the night. It was tradition. The ancient Greeks believed the spirit of the dead escaped through the eyes. It was the least a ventriloquist could do.

Then he opened the wardrobe door to put away the suitcase. There sat the dybbuk at the corner, his neon-lit eyes peering back at Freddie.

"So you bombed again," remarked the spirit.

"What are you doing here?"

"Do we have a deal?"

"What deal?"

"Maybe I can help your act," said the dybbuk. "I know some good jokes. Just allow me to knock around in your skin."

"You mean, be possessed?"

"You'll hardly know I'm there."

"No, thanks. I don't care to have a punk walking around inside my clothes."

"Is that a maybe?"

"That's a firm no," replied the ventriloquist.

"I won't be any trouble. Shall I explain?"

"Beat it!"

The spirit's eyes, suddenly sad, gazed up at him. "You're too busy to give me a listen? Let me tell you about us dybbuks. We all have left something behind among the living. Something unfinished. So what am I doing here? What did I leave undone? A good question. How about my bar mitzvah? But more, too. So I decided to return and fix what needed fixing. I could use your help."

"Why pick on me?"

"Why not you? Didn't you give me a promise, once?"

The Great Freddie sat on the edge of the narrow bed and hunched his shoulders. "I promised you?"

Said the dybbuk, "The German train moving you to another camp—it was wrecked, remember? You were able to escape in the woods. Yes or no, eh? Was the train struck by lightning on a clear night?"

"A handful of men from the underground blew it up."

"Was one of them a boy in a coat down to his ankles? Redheaded?"

"Was that you?"

"Me. In person."

The Great Freddie sat stunned.

The dybbuk's voice fell into a whisper.

"Who led you to the cellar in the bombed-out beer factory to hide from the Germans, you and your dummy in a pillow sack? My own hiding place."

"I remember."

"I remember you made the dummy talk. And then the gang of us showed you the way through the mountains. Did you make it to Switzerland? Before you left, you said, 'I will look for you after the war. I owe you plenty.' And did you look?"

"Yes," said the American. "I found out you were dead."

"True. But surprise. I found you," said the dybbuk. "Last week in Vienna, I saw a flyer with a picture of you and your dummy.

I recognized the dummy. I decided you were the one to help me."

The Great Freddie stood up. "I'm glad that our paths crossed again. I want to help you. But I don't want to be possessed by a Jewish dybbuk. When I was growing up, I never saw a Jew. I thought they all wore horns and had tails."

Said the dybbuk, "What do you know? In the shtetl where I grew up, the muddy village, we thought all Christians had tails and horns. And the Nazi soldiers carried pitchforks."

"I can't help you in this way," said The Great Freddie with genuine regret. "I'm sorry."

"I don't have to ask permission," said the dybbuk. "I know dybbuks who buzz in like houseflies without even knocking. I was just being polite."

CHAPTER

※ 3 ※

From Rome and then across southern France, on train after train, The Great Freddie sat practicing. He knew he moved his lips when he threw his voice. While taking a walk or in the shower, he'd practice with a finger touching his mouth to detect movement. Words with B's in them became words with D's, and M's became N's. Barbarian became dardarian.

Family became fanily. Voice throwers had their own tricks of the tongue.

From town to town, the ventriloquist found himself checking his hotel closets. He had to make sure they were empty before checking in. By the time he reached Marseille, he had money in his pocket again and he felt he'd left the dybbuk somewhere behind. He would like to have helped the ghost kid who had saved him from the Germans, but the kid's request was too weird.

The Great Freddie was booked for the week at the Club Terminus, recently opened across from the railroad station. His leg on a chair, clutching his dummy in the spotlight, he was getting laughs. All went well until the vampire tried to sink his fangs into The Great Freddie's neck. "You can't bite my neck, Count Dracula," he was saying. "You've got no teeth."

He felt a breath of air escape his lips.

"Gefehlt ist gefehlt!" exclaimed the dummy.

That hadn't been the ventriloquist talking. The hair stiffened on the back of his neck. Who was speaking German? Not him.

The Great Freddie struggled to recover his calm. He spoke slowly, as if to double-check every word as it came forth. "I didn't know you speak German," he heard himself say to the dummy. "I hope you didn't join the Nazi Party."

He felt another puff of wind rise from his

throat as the count appeared to answer. "Of course not! What do you take me for? A dummy?"

The audience laughed, followed by a burst of applause. The Great Freddie went nose to nose with the dummy. He felt cold sweat popping out under his starched white shirt. It hadn't been him talking with his lips barely apart. It was the young Jewish kid, throwing his voice. The Great Freddie was possessed by the dybbuk!

He struggled through to the end of his routine, anxious to get off the stage. Once he had escaped the spotlight, he fled in a fury.

Back in his dressing room and alone, he

burst out, "Okay, you smart-ass kid, what do you think you're doing? Where are you?"

"Where do you think?" came the answer from Freddie's own throat, as if he'd swallowed a telephone.

"Get lost!" the ventriloquist growled. "Beat it! I won't have a demon under my skin."

"Who said a demon? That's not kind. A mere dybbuk, I told you. Harmless as a slice of rye bread."

"You're bothering me!" Freddie exclaimed. "Scram! Buzz off!"

Ignoring him, the dybbuk said, "Professor, did you hear the laugh we got? Practically an ovation. Your old routine was so full of moth holes you could strain borscht. How could I resist giving you a hand?"

"Nazis! No one wants to think about the war anymore. It's over."

"Not for me it's over," said the dybbuk. "I have unfinished business."

"Finish it somewhere else."

"But we need each other."

"We, again?" protested the ventriloquist.

"I could be your best friend. I don't see any others hanging around. And I told you, I grew up with actors. Comedians, too. At the age of three I was already performing in Odessa. I can do voices. You want to hear me do Churchill? Roosevelt? The Three

Stooges? I know all the Jewish shtick. The stage business."

"I don't want your Jewish shtick!" said The Great Freddie. "Hit the road!"

"What's the rush?"

"Look, kid—"

"Avrom Amos."

"I've got a date after the show. I don't want a brat like you tagging along!"

"That fake Spanish dancer? I caught her act. She's got feet like woodpeckers. What a noise."

"Did you hear me?"

"You want to be alone? I'll make myself scarce."

"Better than that. Bail out! Beat it!"

At that moment the Greek acrobat came in and looked around. "You talking to someone, Freddie?"

"Talking to myself," replied the ventriloquist, breaking into a sweat.

CHAPTER

⇒ 4 ⇐

It was a balmy night. The Great Freddie and his black-haired dancer stepped out into the street. They found a hole-in-the-wall restaurant for a late bite to eat. It was almost midnight.

"The way you're glancing behind, Freddie, you'd think we were being followed," remarked the Spanish dancer, who had hoop earrings large enough to jump through. She wore a fox fur thrown around her neck, out of season on a warm night.

Freddie picked up the soiled menu. "What'll you have, Consuelo?"

"You order for me," said the dancer, checking her makeup in a compact mirror.

Freddie froze as he felt a puff of air rise from his windpipe. "What's the matter, fräulein? Can't you read anything but German?"

The dybbuk! Consuelo threw an icy glare at Freddie across the small table. "Are you trying to be funny?"

"Funny, no—insulting, yes," replied the dybbuk, crowding out Freddie's own voice.

"Senorita, you're as Spanish as sauerkraut. The way you dance reminds me of German soldiers goose-stepping."

Her face went pale. She stood up, tipping over a glass flower vase. She peered at The Great Freddie with a blaze of contempt. "Are all Americans pigs?" she muttered, and walked out.

Freddie sizzled. He clenched his jaws but managed to speak. "Dybbuk! I'm going to break your Jewish neck, if you have one!"

"I was doing you a favor," the dybbuk replied. "I can smell a German a mile off. She can't hide from me."

"You're loco!"

"She's Nazi rotten. That show-off fox fur

around her neck, biting its own tail. A Spanish lady? No. I saw used clothing like that all over Germany. Stolen. Stripped off the backs of Jewish women pushed alive into the gas chambers. One look at your dancer and I broke into a sweat. She's trying to pass for a Spanish somebody with no blood on her hands."

The Great Freddie ignored the glances from a nearby diner, who must have thought he was mumbling to himself. "What if you're wrong?"

"What if I'm right? That fräulein can't fool me. She's given me so many Nazi salutes she still sleeps with her arm in the air."

Freddie gave his fingers a loud snap. "I'm

through fighting the war. Stop hanging around me! Stop possessing me! Stop talking from my lips! Vanish!"

"You'll feel better in the morning."

"Wanna bet?" Freddie replied. He left a tip on the table and walked out. Bristling, he glanced back, as if he might have left the dybbuk sitting there. Not that cheeky kid. No such luck.

CHAPTER

❖ 5 ❖

At the crack of dawn, Freddie sat through a candlelit mass in a small church a block from his hotel. As soon as the service ended, he stopped the little priest before the holy man could disappear into the shadows.

"Father," said the ventriloquist. "Can you perform an exorcism?"

"You know someone possessed?"

"And how. It's me."

"You may be imagining it," said the priest.

"I'm not imagining anything."

"There is a young priest in Lyon who is talented at plucking out demons by the scruff of the neck. A contribution to the church would be a blessing."

"I could pay something now and the rest later," said Freddie. "I have big show dates coming up in Paris."

The priest folded his arms patiently. "Perhaps it would be enough to mark the sanctified cross on your forehead with holy oil. Tell me about this demon of yours."

"It's a dybbuk."

The priest's arms dropped. "A dybbuk! A Jewish spirit?"

"That's what he says."

The priest broke into a crusty scowl. "My son, are you making a joke? This is a Catholic church. We don't do Jews." And then he smiled. "Go find yourself a rabbi, and Jesus be with you!"

A moment later, Freddie was out on the street, not knowing which way to turn. Were there any Jews left alive in Marseille after the slaughter? Some of the French, defeated by the Germans, had collaborated with the Nazis. They had rounded up their Jewish countrymen and packed them into cattle cars for the death camps.

Freddie stepped in and out of a few shops, asking if anyone could steer him to a synagogue. A butcher peered at him through watery blue eyes and said, "You don't look Jewish."

"You don't look Bulgarian."

"I'm not Bulgarian," replied the butcher defensively.

"I'm not Jewish," Freddie said.

Almost at once, it stung him that he'd bothered to clear himself. That must have been the lonely Nebraska child moving his lips. What had he known about anything? He'd changed adopted parents and religions almost as swiftly as streetcars.

While he had sat on church benches, he

had seen that the denominations barely tolerated one another, but almost all of them despised the Jews. He'd never actually laid eyes on a Jew, but he had kept on the lookout for men with Old Testament beards who were trying to conceal their tails and who wore black hats to hide their horns. He had supposed that even their kids his own age smelled powerfully of brimstone, like boxes of smoldering kitchen matches. He had been relieved to learn that he was merely an orphan, and not a Jew.

Where were all the taxis? He was standing on the curb ready to whistle one down.

Freddie suddenly thought of Bill Billy, his first dummy. He'd carved the head out of a chunk of sugar pine. He had dressed the puppet in bib overalls cut down to size. The nose, painted with red freckles, was a dowel eleven inches long. Like Pinocchio, every time Bill Billy stretched the truth, his nose grew longer.

The puppet had been The Great Freddie's ticket out of the wheat fields of Nebraska. Bill Billy had caught a killer piece of shrapnel during the war. Freddie had buried him in Germany.

A taxi pulled up at last. Freddie leaned forward and told the driver to find him a Jew.

"Any particular Jew?" asked the driver.

"There's more than one?"

"A few are coming back."

"I'm looking for a rabbi."

The taxi driver hesitated and then nodded. "I've seen some work going on in a synagogue in the old port quarter. There may be a rabbi."

When the taxi pulled up at a small, thick-walled building with most of its windows broken out, Freddie took it to have been abandoned during the war. A burst of heavy hammering came echoing from inside.

Freddie saw a wide-shouldered man on a ladder paneling one of the walls. He wore a small, embroidered skullcap, a yarmulke, that seemed to cling to his head by faith alone. He had a young, wispy beard that reminded Freddie of Spanish moss swaying in the breeze. With the man's sleeves rolled up, Freddie could see a string of blue numbers tattooed along his wrist.

Freddie had seen tattoos like that before. The numbers revealed a past of horrors in the German death camps, where the Nazis had branded each Jew with a number that couldn't be washed off. The rabbi had somehow escaped the gas ovens.

"Was this a synagogue?" Freddie asked, peering at the shambles of a building.

"It still is. But not ready for business yet."

"I need to find a rabbi," said Freddie.

"I'm a rabbi. Wait a moment while I hit my thumb again." He finished driving in the nail and climbed down from the ladder.

"Rabbi Moise Bindle," he said, extending his fist of a hand and a smile.

After a shake, Freddie said, "My name is Freddie. Fred T. Birch. I'm an American."

"I noticed."

"I have been possessed by a dybbuk."

"Congratulations," remarked the rabbi, who seemed at ease in the English language. Later, he explained that he'd grown up in Brooklyn.

"I want the dybbuk yanked out," Freddie declared. "Exorcised."

"Who wouldn't? But I have never talked to a dybbuk, face-to-face. They don't hang around street corners, you know. They're rare."

"Not rare enough. This one is a smart-mouthed pest."

Like the priest earlier, the rabbi patiently folded his arms. "*Nu.* Introduce us."

Freddie felt his muscles ease. Now he was getting somewhere. "Dybbuk!" he commanded. "Avrom Amos, meet Rabbi Bindle."

"*Vie gehtz?*" said the rabbi, by way of greeting.

Freddie relaxed his jaw to allow the dybbuk to take over freely. He waited for the faint tickle in his throat. The slight puff of breath. But Avrom Amos had gone hard of hearing.

"Listen, dybbuk. Your rabbi wants to talk to you."

Freddie waited for the now-familiar

blustering voice. But not a word flew from his lips. Not a sound.

"Dybbuk!" he demanded. "Speak up!"

A pin-drop silence.

"Nu?" said the rabbi.

Freddie began to shout. "None of your dybbuk tricks! Talk!"

The rabbi peered at Freddie as if the American might be a lunatic. They waited for several moments more, but the dybbuk had shut up like a clam. The rabbi asked, "Are you sure you have a dybbuk?"

"Positive."

"A shy fellow, eh?"

"Shy as a brass band!"

The rabbi isn't believing me, Freddie

thought. Who could blame him? "Try something, Rabbi. Anything!"

"So you won't go away disappointed, I'll blow the ram's horn. The shofar. If there's a dybbuk, the noise of the ancients should chase him out."

"I'll be obliged," said Freddie, though he wondered if the rabbi was now only humoring him. Probably.

"But without the power of a minyan, who knows?" the rabbi added, as if to qualify the outcome.

"A what?"

"A quorum of ten Jews. Righteous Jews. Good men. Without a minyan, a holy service has no teeth. But you are troubled, and what harm can the shofar do?"

The rabbi unlocked a mahogany cabinet and removed a ram's horn. It glistened, yellow with great age. Returning to Freddie's side, he lifted the shofar to his lips. "You hard of hearing, young American?"

"No."

"You will be." The rabbi held the end of the shofar inches from Freddie's left ear and blew. A wailing blast came forth that almost knocked Freddie off his feet.

"Out, dybbuk!" commanded the rabbi. "Uneasy intruder! Pesky spirit! In the name of the Almighty, flee the body of this nice American. A Gentile. What do you want to bother him for? Come a little closer, dybbuk, and listen. I, Moise, son of Isaac, son of Yankel, command you to obey. Jump out! Run for the good of your soul. Refuse and I will fill you like a pincushion with curses and oaths and painful maledictions! Are you listening, dybbuk? I command you to harm no living creature, especially this American! Leap out, and I will reward you with blessings and forgive the troubled mischief that drives you. Nu? Agreed? *Baruch atah . . .*"

Finishing the Hebrew prayer, the rabbi lifted the ram's horn to Freddie's ear and blew. Once more, the ventriloquist felt as if he'd been hit with a two-by-four.

Freddie peeled off French francs to help

the rabbi rebuild the synagogue, and soon was flagging down a taxi.

He felt buoyant. He was eager to believe the whole whoop-de-doodle had worked. Maybe the dybbuk had been scared out of his skin by the ancient blast of the ram's horn and had left without saying good-bye.

Once Freddie was back in the small elevator of his hotel, a familiar voice burst into the air. "The ram's horn! That wasn't a friendly thing to do!"

"You're back!" Freddie exclaimed.

"I was never gone," said the dybbuk.

"What do I have to do to get rid of you?"

"Try chicken soup."

CHAPTER
✦ 6 ✦

The passing rain had turned the streets of Paris into a scattering of broken mirrors. Black umbrellas had sprouted like mushrooms. It was already spring.

But a frost had settled in the theatrical office where Freddie sat across the desk from the gravel-voiced man who found him work. Viktor Chambrun had himself been a performer, a baggy-pants comic. After losing an arm in the war, he'd become an agent in Paris, booking other acts across Europe.

"Sorry, kid," said the agent, his voice rasping like a file. "You've been canceled at the Crazy Horse."

"Why?" asked Freddie, startled. He was counting on the Crazy Horse to give him a leg up into the big time. It was a popular tourist cabaret.

"The director booked another ventriloquist. One who doesn't move his lips."

"But my Count Dracula routine is a hit."

"Where? Transylvania?" With his remaining arm, the agent lit a cigar. "I'll get you a spot in one of the cellar clubs. At least you'll eat. You're not ready for the top spots. And that vampire is about as funny as indigestion. Sometimes I wonder if you were cut out to be a straight man to a piece of wood, Freddie."

"I hold my own."

"Maybe it's time you went home. The war's over, soldier."

"I'm not giving up on the Crazy Horse," said Freddie firmly. Now he regarded it as Mount Everest. He wanted to climb to the top.

Freddie left, dismayed and angry. Go home to what? A sunburned neck in the wheat fields? He wandered the misty streets. Now the black umbrellas made him wonder if all Paris was going to a funeral. He sat down at a sidewalk café and ordered a black coffee.

He felt a tickle of breath. "I heard," said the dybbuk, in a voice that seemed to rise from Freddie's stomach.

"I don't need your sympathy," Freddie replied.

"Who's giving it? You want to play the Crazy Horse? I'll fix it."

"Get lost."

"Shlemiel. Let me do the talking."

"I can't shut you up."

"Shmendrik. Let me talk in the act. You won't have to move your lips."

Freddie jerked up his head. "What did you say?"

"I said—"

"Never mind. I heard you. Can you talk through my nose?"

"Easy."

"Then I could tape my lips shut."

"You could drink a bottle of Perrier."

"While the count is talking a mile a minute."

"Two miles."

"We'll be a sensation!" Freddie exclaimed, rising to his feet. "Come on."

"Where?"

"Mount Everest."

CHAPTER

❖ 7 ❖

The Great Freddie broke in his new act on the Left Bank at a small theater around the corner from the Sorbonne University.

"Ready?" he muttered. "You know your lines?"

"Backward," replied the dybbuk. "Break a leg, Professor."

It was a show-business prayer for a good

performance, and it now floated inside Freddie's head. He took the spotlight and sat the dummy on his knee.

"Count," he said. "I'm thirsty. Why don't you recite the alphabet while I have a drink of water?"

"Shoot," said the dummy. "Aleph, bet, gimmel . . ."

"The English alphabet, if you don't mind. A, B, C—"

"D, E, F—"

Freddie picked up a bottle of Perrier water and began to drink.

"G, H, I—"

The sound of scattered applause, like a flight of pigeons, arose from the theater. It quickly thickened as astonishment grew. How was the ventriloquist doing it? His lips couldn't move. They were clamped to the Perrier.

The Great Freddie put down the bottle to a furnace blast of applause.

"Not bad," the count remarked.

The Great Freddie shrugged. "What if I were to tape my mouth?"

"Quite impossible!" declared the dummy.

"Quite astonishing, pal."

The ventriloquist slapped adhesive tape over his mouth until his lower face looked as wrapped as a mummy.

"What a show-off!" shouted the wooden puppet. "You and your cheap tricks. Just don't ask me to whistle!"

Almost at once, the dummy began to whistle and the audience burst into another thunderclap of applause.

Said the dybbuk, "Look at The Great Freddie. He's going to have to peel that tape off his skin. Ouch! Now, I ask you. Which one is the dummy?"

The Great Freddie was a hit!

Word quickly got around Paris that an American ventriloquist was throwing his voice with his lips sealed with tape or while drinking a bottle of Perrier. Theaters clamored for The Great Freddie. Overnight, he had become a star attraction.

The gloom in his agent's office had lifted.

"The Crazy Horse?" declared Viktor, his gravel voice rattling. "The longer we make 'em wait for The Great Freddie, the more they'll pay. I've already got you booked around town for the next couple of months. That'll give you time to polish your material and get some class. Here's a fistful of francs to tide you over. Buy yourself a new suit of tails and a flower for your buttonhole."

Freddie moved to the old Grand Hotel, a big barn of a place in the center of Paris. Night after night, Freddie stepped into the spotlight in outlying theaters and cabarets. The dybbuk was a natural. He knew how to get laughs. Sometimes he seemed to amuse himself by changing voices. One night the dummy might speak with a Hungarian accent; another night, Polish.

But trouble loomed.

At a late Friday breakfast, the dybbuk said, "Mr. Big-Shot Ventriloquist, I'm not going on tonight."

"What are you talking about? We're booked."

"It's Friday."

"Yes. Friday turns up every week."

Said the dybbuk, "It's Shabbes. The Sabbath. When the Friday sun sets, the holiday arrives. On Shabbes, I don't work."

"But you must!"

"On the holy day, Jews don't lift a finger. Not until the sun sets on Saturday. So, no matinee shows. You'll have to do the act without me."

Freddie felt a wave of distress. "People come to see me drink a bottle of water!"

"I don't lift a finger."

"I'll get booed off the stage."

"Gut Shabbes."

"What do you expect me to do?"

"Tell 'em to come back Saturday after the sun sets."

For a week, Freddie barely spoke to the dybbuk except on stage. He had to cancel all Friday night performances and all Saturday matinees. Viktor almost choked on his cigar. But how could Freddie tell him that a dybbuk was doing the talking?

After a few weeks, word got around that The Great Freddie wouldn't work Friday nights or Saturday afternoons.

"Do you know that gossip has sprung up?" Freddie reported. "Theater managers are wondering if I'm Jewish."

"Oy, such a crime," said the dybbuk.

"But I'm not!"

"That's not a crime either."

"You could do me a big favor. Show up Friday night and put an end to the gossip!"

Replied the dybbuk, "I don't lift a finger on Shabbes."

CHAPTER

☀ 8 ☀

Freddie awoke in the night. He had been quietly sobbing in his sleep. What had he to be so sad about? Then he realized it wasn't him. It was the dybbuk softly, softly crying.

Freddie turned on his side, and the sobbing stopped.

The next morning he went to a tailor. He had knockabout clothes made for the dummy, to be more in keeping with its new voice and saucy character.

Freddie said nothing about the sobbing in the night. A flashback to some terror of the kid's war? He forgave his young partner for refusing to work on the Shabbes, as even he now called the weekend holidays. But he was quite unprepared for the favor Avrom Amos was soon to ask. The dybbuk sprang it on a Tuesday as they settled under the spotlight and began their midnight performance.

"Is it true that you've decided to become a vampire and bite people on the neck?" asked the ventriloquist, script perfect.

The dummy replied, "Who do you think I am? Count Dracula?"

That wasn't the right line. Freddie twisted the dummy's head sharply stage left. Eye to eye. Was the dybbuk rewriting the script?

"I said, you've decided to become a vampire."

"Not me," remarked the puppet. "Blood-sucking I leave to the Nazis."

This was no place for the dybbuk to speak his mind. But Freddie sensed there'd be no shutting off this burst of anger. He considered walking off, but that would create a backstage scandal. Who would hire him again after a stumble like that? There was only one thing to do—give the dybbuk his head. After all, it was a late Tuesday show; not a big night.

"If you're not Count Dracula, who are you?"

"A dybbuk."

Freddie gulped. Was Avrom Amos cueing him? "A dybbuk? What's that?"

"A Jewish spirit."

"Is that like a ghost?"

"Third cousins."

"I've never heard of a ghost in a striped sweater," said Freddie.

"Remember the war, Professor? Heaven is so full of new arrivals, their toes are sticking out the windows. The place ran out of white sheets. Us brats had to take whatever we could find."

"You're a child?"

"Why not? Millions of us Jewish kids up there."

The Great Freddie paused to get a fresh grip on himself. They weren't getting any laughs. Still, the audience was listening. It was not every day they heard a ghost talk.

"If you're a dybbuk, how come you don't smell of brimstone and fire?"

"Why should I?"

"I don't believe you dropped in from the sky."

"Why not?"

"Everyone knows you have to accept Jesus to go to Heaven, and that lets you out. You know that Jews are doomed to go to Hell."

"Have you talked to any eyewitnesses

lately?" replied the dybbuk. "Heaven is packed with Jews. Like sardines. The door is always open. Any nice person can walk in. Like me."

"Says you."

"I heard there was a Christian heaven around the corner. And for Muslims, paradise? A big place with palm trees, down the road."

"Are you trying to be funny?" asked Freddie.

"Funny, Mr. Yankel Doodle?"

"That's Yankee Doodle."

"You want jokes straight from the clouds? Why did the Almighty give food to the rich and an appetite to the poor?"

At last, a nervous laugh erupted.

Said the dummy, "Did I tell you about the time I threw a rope to a drowning Nazi general?"

"That was a Christian thing to do."

"Jewish, too. I threw him both ends."

A bigger laugh came roaring up from the seats. But Heaven, and now Nazi generals! The act was on thin ice. Freddie needed to regain control. To get back to the script.

He picked up the bottle of water. "Care to do something entertaining while I have a long drink?"

"You like to see my war wounds? I've got so many bullet holes you could look through me and see the Eiffel Tower."

"Some other time. Maybe you'd better sing a tune. How about 'Song Without Words'?"

"I don't know the verse," said the dybbuk.

"Just whistle."

The Great Freddie lifted the bottle to his lips. The dummy bent his head back and the dybbuk began to whistle.

The trick brought down the house. The Great Freddie broke into a farm-boy smile. Whaddya know? They went for the dybbuk. Freddie and the wooden dummy took a relieved bow.

"Nice going, Avrom Amos," the ventriloquist said as they reached the wings. "You stay in the act."

CHAPTER

❖ 9 ❖

The Great Freddie kept adding tricks. He'd clamp an apple between his teeth. He stuffed his mouth with a yard of red silk. He gargled ginger ale. Nothing could keep Count Dracula from talking.

Between Thursday night performances, a reporter from *Le Monde*, a Paris newspaper, showed up in his dressing room. She wore a stylish muffler wrapped around her neck in coils like a python. She pulled a yellow pencil out of her frizz of hair and set to work.

"M'sieu Freddie, where did you get ze idea for ze dybbuk in your act? Extraordinaire!"

Freddie cleared his throat to give himself an extra moment before answering. "The idea just grabbed hold of me, you might say."

"Ze dybbuk is a child, no?"

"Yes. I'll let him speak for himself, mademoiselle."

Freddie picked up the puppet and gave its head stick a turn to face the Frenchwoman.

"Nu?" said the dybbuk.

"May I ask how you were presumably killed?" asked the reporter.

"In the usual way. With a gun. And what do you mean, presumably? You think I'm making this up?"

She gave a small laugh. "But of course. It's show biz, no?"

"No," Freddie put in. "It's life."

"True?"

Said the puppet, "I was the last Jew left alive in Olyk."

"Where?"

"Between Lvov and Rovno, in southern Russia. The Ukraine."

"I'll look it up," said the reporter, tongue in cheek, making a note.

"Look up August 22, 1944," said the dybbuk. "That was one of the special days a certain SS officer in his vulture black uniform had put aside to hunt Jewkids, as he called us. He and his men regarded it as a national sport. Children, they'd snatch us out of yards. Infants, from the arms of our mothers. The soldiers knotted us in sacks and heaved us like potatoes onto trucks. The trucks took us to the cattle cars and then it was a free trip for Jewbrats to the death camps. You're not taking notes."

The reporter ignored his comment. "You remember all zis? A piece of firewood?"

"Yes, me, dodging Colonel Junker-Strupp for two years, sometimes dyeing my red hair, hiding like a chameleon among the Aryans. I joined the underground to blow up train tracks and spit at the Nazis. The colonel, smoking his Egyptian cigarettes, came to know about me.

"But that day, in Olyk, my luck went kaput. German soldiers on motorcycles were chasing us, me and my nine-year-old sister, Sulka. We found haystacks to hide in. The soldiers flushed her out. Sulka ran like a mouse, but she was caught by the hair. They killed her on the spot. Another Jewbrat less for Germany. As soon as I felt safe, I slipped away."

"To where?"

"My village. I knew better hiding places than a haystack. A dog began to bark and follow me. Soon a Jew hunter saw us. Finally

German soldiers and the Ukrainian police were chasing me through the lanes. And my neighbors in the village, hearing such a commotion, joined in to rid themselves of vermin like me. I remember yelling back over my shoulder, 'Dear sirs, let me go home to my mother! Dear sirs, let me go home!' My mother was already dead, but I hoped to soften a few Ukrainian hearts. Our old neighbors. Hah! Their hearts were tangles of vipers."

The reporter peered at the ventriloquist. "Alors, that's more make-believe than I need for my article, no?"

Freddie gave a snort. "Make-believe? Trust me. The story is true."

The reporter shot back sarcastically. "But of course! You're saying someone actually murdered zis carved hunk of wood?"

"Six bullet holes," said the dybbuk. "Colonel Junker-Strupp blocked the lane in his Mercedes open car. He stood, smoking a cigarette, a Luger pistol in one hand. There I came, around the corner, the mob after me. I was blocked. I picked up a stone and heaved it at the vulture.

"'With the compliments of Colonel Gerhard Junker-Strupp,' he said, and shot. Quick! *Schnell!* No second thoughts. The bullet spun me around like a top. He emptied his pistol. He left me in the street, bleeding from six holes, the last Jew in Olyk."

SID FLEISCHMAN

"Mon Dieu! A wooden dummy bleeding in ze street?" With a roll of her eyes, the reporter closed her notebook. "Am I to believe a real live demon hides under zees clothes—when it is you doing all the talking, M'sieu Freddie? I do compliment you. I couldn't see you move your lips at all!"

That night the dybbuk sobbed in his sleep. Freddie awoke and let him cry. He had to remind himself that he was possessed by a mere child. The dybbuk's scorn and bluster were grown-up battle wounds.

CHAPTER

❖ 10 ❖

By the time the act opened at the Crazy Horse, Freddie had forgotten why dybbuks chose to leave their graves. But Avrom Amos had not forgotten.

"A small favor? Can I ask?" the dybbuk muttered. Freddie was facing the mirror to apply makeup for the first show of the evening.

"When you say small, I duck."

"Remember, the Germans killed me? Two weeks before my bar mitzvah?"

"You mentioned it," said Freddie.

"You know what is a bar mitzvah?"

"A ceremony of some sort."

"To be declared a man among Jews, a boy must have his bar mitzvah when his thirteenth birthday arrives. By then, my parents were dead. My sisters and little brother— even I was dead."

"Yes. I'm sorry, Avrom Amos."

"I told you dybbuks return to finish something left undone among the living. But it's not too late."

"For what?"

"My birthday is coming up. I want you to fix up my bar mitzvah."

"Ah. So that's why you possessed me!"

Said the dybbuk, "Not exactly. But it's a start."

"For what?"

The dybbuk ignored him. "Listen. For what I came back to do, I need to be a man. A mensch. It's not for a boy in short pants."

"So you need a rabbi or someone to declare you a grown-up—is that it?"

Freddie could almost sense the dybbuk giving a shrug. Avrom Amos said, "Can you imagine a dybbuk walking into a synagogue and saying, 'Rabbi, I just dropped in from the sky. How about a bar mitzvah?' The rabbi would strike his head and shout, 'Meshugge! Crazy! Out!' That's why I need you."

Freddie now felt on guard. "For what, exactly?"

"You walk into the synagogue and let me do the talking."

"Stand in for you?"

"That's the idea."

"But I don't look thirteen!"

"It doesn't matter. Older, even, is okay. Do you think I am thirteen? I feel I have grown a hundred years older."

"And I'm not Jewish!"

"You don't have to shout," said the dybbuk.

"I'd like to help. But count me out."

Said the dybbuk, "You may have noticed, Professor. I stand in for you."

Freddie asked himself if he'd ever won an argument with his new partner. He had a feeling he was going to lose this one. He needed the dybbuk in the act. How would he pull off his great tricks without Avrom Amos?

He finished dressing. "Okay." He sighed. "But don't expect me to wear one of those funny hats."

"It's a package deal," said the dybbuk. "I guarantee nothing."

CHAPTER

⇒ 11 ⇐

Freddie ran into a former girlfriend at his agent's office. Their old romance quickly burst into flames.

Playing small parts in French-made films, Polly Marchant was a showgirl from the American South. She was bouncy and bright and given to making faces. Polly could cross her eyes. She'd muss her blond hair when she felt like it. She had changed little since they had broken up the year before, though now she wore her hair cut short and as tight as a bathing cap.

They began to joke about getting married. Nothing serious. Joking. Polly confessed that she had announced in her diary that she had fallen madly in love, if he'd care to peek. Freddie didn't keep a diary, but his face announced it to the world.

The dybbuk had little patience with the flirtatious sweet talk he heard. He could do voices, and occasionally dropped in a comment from the cowboy actor Gary Cooper. "Yup. Yup. Yup." He abandoned Freddie for hours a day, mumbling to himself as he brushed up on his Hebrew. And he needed to go over the prayers he remembered from the past. *Baruch atah Adonai . . .* He would have to read out of the Torah scroll, something from the first five books of the Bible. But memory wasn't enough. He'd need last-minute schooling. Some polishing.

On his dates with Polly, Freddie was glad to find himself free of the dybbuk. The two Americans were walking along the Champs Elysée when she said, "Darling boy, why didn't you tell me you were Jewish?"

He stopped short. "Where did you get that idea?"

"I do declare, everyone knows it. You

won't work on the Sabbath. And that Jewish dybbuk you use in your act. Of course it's nothing to be ashamed of."

"I'm not ashamed. I'm not Jewish."

"You don't have to hide it from me," she assured him.

"I'm not hiding anything."

"On the level?"

"I promise you."

"How disappointing!" Polly exclaimed. "Can you imagine me dragging a Jewish husband home to Alabama? Wow!" She crossed her eyes. "Some of our redneck neighbors would haul out the tar and feathers."

"I'm one-eighth Cheyenne. Won't that do?"

On the following afternoon, the dybbuk asked Freddie to accompany him to the cheder, a Hebrew school he'd located near the Eiffel Tower.

"I'll wait out here," Freddie said firmly.

"That won't work," said the dybbuk. "Just let me do the talking."

"I'll be a fish out of water," Freddie protested.

"Pretend you're a pickled herring."

The Hebrew teacher, the melamed, was an Algerian Jew with eyes as dark as fire pits. The Great Freddie was quickly registered as Avrom Amos Poliakov. A small school chair at a small desk became his. "Sit, and pay attention," said the melamed.

"I have lost my yarmulke," Freddie heard himself say. What was that? My what? The teacher dug out a small black skullcap. Freddie slapped it on his head and cursed the dybbuk under his breath. The lesson began with a prayer.

"Baruch atah Adonai . . ."

Inwardly, Freddie crossed his arms and tried to tune out.

"Reb Poliakov," said the teacher as they finished the hour. "I notice you don't move your mouth when you repeat after me."

"I never move my lips. I'm a ventriloquist."

After three weeks of listening to the dybbuk's struggle with the Torah, Freddie discovered that a phrase or two was stuck inside his head.

"*Baruch atah Adonai . . . Shema Yisrael . . .*"

Finally, just before they were to go on for the 9:30 show, Freddie muttered to the dybbuk, "What's playing inside my head like a phonograph record? What am I saying?"

"Don't lose any sleep. It's not your bar mitzvah."

"I could be cursing my best friend."

"I'm your best friend."

They approached the wings of the stage and waited for the curtains to part. "So what do the words mean?"

"You're asking God to listen to you," the dybbuk said. "It starts every prayer. So, as the

Torah says, '*Shema Yisrael*, let us break a leg.'"

Freddie laughed. He'd never heard the show-business prayer delivered with ancient Hebrew thrown in. That should guarantee a nifty performance.

CHAPTER

✦ 12 ✦

Summer was settling in. An early dusk, pumpkin tinted, lit the Paris streets like the flare of a match. The sidewalk tables were filling up. Freddie, in a rush along a narrow side street, passed a neighborhood café. A ragged boy in a coat with bulging pockets stood at the window looking in. Freddie barely spared him a glance.

"Stop," said the dybbuk.

"What now? We'll be late for our show."

"The world will end? Don't you rich Americans have eyes?"

"What are you talking about?" Freddie asked.

"That kid at the window. He's hungry."

"How can you tell?"

"What's he looking at inside? Suits, the latest styles? His stomach is growling."

"You heard it?"

"I can hear an empty stomach at ten kilometers. And see how his pockets are bulging? He has everything he owns in those pockets. Give him a few francs so he can eat."

"Avrom, what do you want me to do, feed every street kid and beggar in Paris?"

"Why not?"

"We're going to miss our curtain."

"Let them hold the curtain," said the dybbuk. "If you can't spare a few francs, take it out of my account."

"What account?" Freddie replied scornfully. He supposed Avrom Amos was seeing himself hungry at a café window, with everything he possessed in the world stuffed inside his pockets.

Freddie dug wrinkled paper francs out of his pocket and shoved them into the hand of the street kid.

"Here. Get something to eat."

When Freddie reached the Crazy Horse, and after hastily pinning a fresh flower in the buttonhole of his tailcoat, he strode center stage. The curtains parted. He rested a polished black shoe on a chair and sat the dummy on his knee.

The puppet looked at him. "Do I know you?"

Here we go, thought the ventriloquist. "I'm The Great Freddie."

"What makes you so great?"

"I can throw my voice upstage into that barrel."

"You get paid for throwing up?"

"I didn't say that," protested The Great Freddie. "I can toss my voice anywhere."

SID FLEISCHMAN

"How about my pocket?"

"What do you want your pocket to say?"

"Keep out!"

"Why are you all dressed up?" Freddie hoped to get the dialogue back on track. "Aren't you Count Dracula?"

"That shlemiel of a vampire? I'm a dybbuk."

"A what?"

"A nice Jewish demon. I haunt people."

"That doesn't sound nice to me."

"Is fighting wars nice?" replied the dybbuk.

"The war's history. Yesterday's newspapers."

"Not for me. I placed a want ad. Let me look at the audience."

"Are you searching for a friend?"

"A rat."

"There are no rodents in this cabaret," Freddie said. Where was this dialogue going?

The dybbuk said, "Keep your eyes peeled for a rat with two legs."

"An unfortunate pet? Did you name him?"

"No. He already had a name."

"What was it?"

"SS Colonel Gerhard Junker-Strupp. You've heard of him?"

"No."

"Aha!"

"What do you mean, aha?"

"He was the worst of the Jewish child

killers, and you've never heard of him."

"I have a feeling this is something personal."

"He caught me. He shot me, personally."

"I hope you find him," said Freddie, eager to change the subject. "What do you know about vampires?"

"Vampires are a pain in the neck."

"Yes."

"I think I'll buy a pair of platypuses," the dybbuk continued.

"Why on earth would you want a pair of platypuses?"

"Because they're so hard for a ventriloquist to say without moving his lips. Hey, you did good, Professor!"

Applause, at last. Freddie survived the act somehow, took a brisk bow, and fled the stage. He put the dummy away for the night, forgetting to cover its eyes with the black cloth.

What was it with the dybbuk? This was show business. No place to get even with the Nazis. It was now clear why Avrom Amos Poliakov had chosen a ventriloquist to possess. To play the mouthpiece. To bear witness.

CHAPTER

⇢ 13 ⇠

The dybbuk's Saturday-morning bar mitzvah struck Freddie as an untranslated page of the Bible. He hardly understood a word being said in the synagogue. So this was the ancient language Moses had spoken. It sounded heavy with Old Testament cobwebs. Mercifully, the ceremony took less than an hour.

A minyan of bearded Jews hung around

him while he stood at the open scroll of the Torah. The dybbuk began to read his appointed text. Freddie moved his lips so that he might appear to be talking. For the first time, he felt like one of his own wooden dummies.

Freddie had bought a dark suit for the occasion. Now he'd put the yarmulke on his head, and a prayer shawl over his shoulders. He looked neither left nor right. He was an imposter. He looked down.

He felt profoundly disappointed for the dybbuk. Where were his parents? His sisters? His little brother? His aunts and uncles and cousins to make it a celebration? Freddie was his only family and friend.

Finally the dybbuk gave a sort of curtain speech. It was brief.

"Now that I am a man, I will conduct myself as a mensch," he said to the congregation of strangers. "While a child I saw enough blood to overflow the Red Sea. I saw Germans set Jewish beards like yours on fire, and laugh. I hid in sewers. Now I will wish peaceful lives for you all. But not for the Nazis. Not for SS Colonel Gerhard Junker-Strupp. It will be his turn to hide in the sewers."

Him again, Freddie thought. The child killer. Avrom Amos's own murderer.

The dybbuk fell silent. The ceremony was finished. Freddie didn't have to be told. He could head for the heavy synagogue doors.

"Mazel tov!" came a happy fireworks of voices.

"What does that shout mean?" Freddie asked, once they were out on the sidewalk.

"Congratulations."

"Then, *mazel tov*, now that you are officially a man. With that unfinished business wrapped up, I suppose you'll pack and head for the clouds, or wherever you came from."

"I'm not finished. Now I can deal with the SS child butcher."

Freddie whistled for a taxi. "You can't be serious. That German officer was probably killed in the war."

"Not him."

"Why did you wait so long to start searching?"

"Do you think I've been twiddling my thumbs since the war? There's no school for dybbuks, you know, to teach us shlemiels all the tricks. It took me a year to track him to Warsaw and another year plus to find his footprints in Berlin. That's when SS Officer Junker-Strupp disappeared."

"Vanished?"

"Slipped out of Germany, like other war criminals."

"To South America?"

"I think he's still in Europe. How cunning he was to get himself tattooed! On his forearm."

Said Freddie, "Not numbers!"

"Yes, numbers. Like a concentration-camp survivor. Who would look for him among Jews?"

"Nazi cunning," Freddie muttered.

"But I'm cunning, too."

"I have noticed."

"I tracked down the German corporal who tattooed him. I got the number. I will track down the counterfeit Jew with J117722 on his right wrist."

"And then what?"

"I will kill him," said the dybbuk.

The taxi blew its horn at a child racing across the street. The dybbuk didn't mutter another word. But once they swung around the Arc de Triomphe, Freddie said, "That's crazy."

"Did I say it wasn't?"

"How do you think you can kill him? You haven't enough substance to lift a knife or pull a trigger."

"True. But there is a way."

"What's that?"

"You can pull the trigger for me."

Freddie leaned forward and told the taxi driver to stop, surprising a flutter of pigeons. "This is where I get out," Freddie said, and threw open the door.

"Wait. I'll come with you," said the dyb-buk.

CHAPTER

❖ 14 ❖

The Crazy Horse was befogged with cigarette smoke. The showgirls, high kicking, arms locked like a chain of paper dolls, vanished one by one into the wings. There stood The Great Freddie, glum faced, waiting to go on.

The dybbuk had fallen silent since breakfast. He wasn't apt to show up. Freddie could already feel the flop sweat; he'd be standing unmasked in the spotlight. He couldn't throw his voice without moving his lips—like a carp, the dybbuk had once remarked. The shtick was out. He'd have to cut the bottle of Perrier. Forget taping his lips. Once again, he was a so-so ventriloquist.

What choice do you have, Freddie? he asked himself sullenly. Can't let the dybbuk blackmail you into committing a murder. Not a chance. Nope. "But in the army, they taught you to kill," the dybbuk had said at breakfast. "When you dropped bombs, do you think people didn't die?"

"That was war. You can't kill the German officer without a trial."

"Did he give me judge and jury?"

With a decisive chop of his hand, Freddie had said, "I'm not going to be a bloody barbarian because he was a bloody barbarian. It's no deal."

The dybbuk had fallen silent.

The walk-on music penetrated Freddie's thoughts. He left the safety of the wings and found himself blinded by the spotlight. The audience sat unseen in the dark. What shambles of the act did he have left? Who was the puppet to be now? A schoolboy?

"What do you like best about school?" the ventriloquist asked.

"When it's closed," the dummy answered.

The laughs were polite. That was the kiss

of death, Freddie knew. He racked his brain for better material—any old stuff.

"Did you say you hate dogs?" he asked the wooden puppet.

"I didn't, but I do."

"Why do you hate dogs?"

There came a pause. "You're forgetting. I was once a tree, Professor." That wasn't Freddie himself throwing the punch line.

It was the dybbuk!

A big laugh broke from the audience, and a smile rose like a sunrise across Freddie's face. His partner, his friend, was back!

He picked up the pace, eager to steer the material to familiar terrain. "Why are you wearing short pants?" he asked.

"It's a long story."

"Make it brief."

"I'm a dybbuk."

The Great Freddie was back in business.

CHAPTER
⇒ 15 ⇐

"Thanks, pal. Thanks, Avrom." Freddie said once they were back in the dressing room.

"So now we're on a first name, huh?"

"I was dying out there."

"I saw," replied the dybbuk.

"But I haven't changed my mind about knocking off that German for you."

Said the dybbuk, "And me? When I was a

kid, my mind was on an eye for an eye. Now I am bar mitzvahed. I am now a man. How would a mensch behave? So I changed my mind."

"What are you going to do?"

"Drive him crazy. Leave it to me," said the dybbuk.

Freddie offered up a smile. "I won't bet against you, Avrom."

"Now, may I suggest—buy her flowers."

"What?"

"So upset you were with me, you forgot to keep your date for lunch. Polly."

Freddie picked out an armful of firecracker-red snapdragons and had them sent to Polly's hotel. The next day, he waited at an outside table at Maxim's. She came clicking along on heels as tall as telephone poles.

He pulled back a chair. "Sit down," he said.

She gave him an onionskin smile, thin and dry. "I won't ask you to tell me why you stood me up."

"Good. Then I won't have to lie, because you'd never believe me."

She sat down and crossed her legs. Now he could see the flames of a bonfire building up in her eyes. Before each word left her lips, she dipped it in a southern accent, thick as gravy. "I declare if you don't take me for a belle with boll weevils in her hair. Think I don't know B from buckshot? I know when I'm being lied to, honey. What does a country girl like me need with a traveling man like you who doesn't level with her?"

Freddie stared at her, bewildered. "Do I know what you're talking about?"

"I got the goods on you. You fibbed to me. You lied. You're Jewish as a bagel. You should have leveled with me. What's wrong with being a Jewboy?"

"Sensitively put," Freddie declared sharply.

"Then why don't you put me down? Where's your backbone?"

"I did level with you. I'm not Jewish."

"Liar!"

"We had this out once before. You don't
know B from buckshot."

"Ha!" Her voice rose an octave. "Shut my
mouth, or shut yours! I got wised up! You
snuck into the synagogue and got that bar
mitzvah thing done. You're lying in my face."

He fumbled for something to say. His
head spun. "That wasn't me, Polly!"

"You got a twin? One of the bit players
from my film was there in the synagogue. He
saw you."

Freddie gazed at her. His mouth fell open
like a hooked bass. There seemed to be no air
in his lungs. How could he tell her he had
only stood in for a dybbuk? That he was possessed by a demon? She'd take him for a

The Entertainer and the Dybbuk

genuine nut. There was just so much that romance could bear.

He gazed at her a long time, and she waited. Finally he said, "Okay. You got me, Polly. I'm one of the chosen people."

CHAPTER
✦ 16 ✦

The Great Freddie was held over at the Crazy Horse for seven weeks. The dybbuk lost no opportunity while in the spotlight to pursue the German SS officer. He'd know the vulture even out of uniform.

"Can I tack up a wanted poster now?" asked the dummy.

Freddie was taken by surprise. "What

wanted poster? The Nazi child killer?"

"That's him."

"But you said he changed his name."

"Look for the number on his wrist—
J117722. He probably hangs around stamp
shows."

"How do you know?" It never failed to
surprise Freddie that audiences sat still for the
dybbuk's broadsides.

"If you had trunks full of stolen stamps,
where would you go? To church?"

Freddie was aware that the war had
turned Germany into a country of muggers
and housebreakers. Silver candlesticks,
paintings off the walls, jewels—nothing the
Jews owned was safe from grab-and-steal by

their fellow Germans, not even gold teeth.

"So your Colonel Junker-Strupp had an eye for grabbing stamp collections," The Great Freddie remarked. "And if he's on the run, he'd need to raise cash by selling off rare stamps."

"Aha!" exclaimed the dybbuk. "My plan exactly."

"What plan?"

"To track down the stamp collector. Mr. Freddie, take my advice and hold on to your socks."

"Why?"

"Because, what I got to say, you're going to jump out of your socks in front of the whole audience."

"I doubt it."

"You remember SS Colonel Gerhard Junker-Strupp? Maybe someone has seen him. I am offering a cash reward!"

"A what?"

Not only did Freddie come close to jumping out of his socks, but his glistening patent-leather shoes, as well. After a moment to collect himself, he said, "You don't have any money for a reward. Not a franc to your name."

"But you do."

The audience roared out a laugh.

Almost at once when they reached the dressing room, Freddie folded his arms. He gazed hard into the mirror as if he could see the dybbuk through the glass. "So now I am to pay your reward if anyone actually finds the German."

"Why not? Have I ever asked for a franc? A mark? A ruble? Am I slave labor?"

Freddie immediately felt on the defensive. "It never occurred to me that you needed money. Where would you keep your francs and marks and rubles? In my pocket?"

"Just don't get your pocket picked," said the dybbuk, dismissing the matter.

At every performance, Avrom Amos refreshed the details. The former SS colonel had a nose as sharp as a meat cleaver. He bit his nails. He smoked Egyptian cigarettes. He had so many dueling scars, he looked as if he had plaid cheeks. His eyes were a pale and ghostly blue.

If Freddie had resented the dybbuk's choosing to possess him, he had to hand it to the kid. The stage was Avrom Amos's billboard. He would spread the news, like a village crier, and he might find his murderer.

Might. While Freddie said nothing to discourage the dybbuk, he figured that a needle in a haystack would be easier to turn up.

Night after night, audience after audience, the needle was not found.

Meanwhile, Polly could generally be seen hanging on to Freddie's arm. She was already bubbling with plans.

"Of course we'll have a Jewish wedding,"

she said. "Don't you think we'll look heavenly under that canopy thing? And you'll have to stamp on the wineglass in a silk handkerchief. I wonder if it's filled with wine. We'll want a good year. Maybe a Lafitte Rothschild."

"You've been reading up," said Freddie, both amused and dismayed. He was feeling more and more like an imposter. How could he marry her with a dybbuk under his skin? She'd scream her southern head off if she found out there were three of them on the honeymoon. "No need to rush things," he said.

"Of course, there is, you darling man," she exclaimed. "Love? Have you heard of it?

We'll make a quick trip home to meet the family. Wait until my uncle Wimble in Mobile lays eyes on a Jew. He's the family Klansman. He'll have a heart attack! It'll do him good."

CHAPTER

❖ 17 ❖

It was while shaving that Freddie told the dybbuk for the first time that sometimes he could be heard crying in his sleep.

"It's against the law?" replied the dybbuk. He sounded surprised.

"I'm sure you have plenty to give you nightmares. Sulka was your sister, wasn't she?"

The dybbuk was slow to answer. "I spoke her name in my sleep?"

"Every night."

"I saw how they killed her. Did I tell you?"

"No."

"Why waste good German bullets on trashy little Jews, eh? The Nazis figured out a new way to rid Europe of us vermin. It was cheaper to rub poison on our lips, the lips of kids and babies.

"I saw it with my own eyes, on the road from Lvov, SS men on motorcycles chasing Sulka and me. We hid in a ditch and then burrowed like mice into moldy haystacks."

"You told me."

"Sulka had lost a shoe running in the mud and the vultures followed her one-shoe footprints. They pulled her from her hiding place and burst out laughing like shikkers."

"Shikkers?"

"Drunks. They were SS child killers. They got a thick glass bottle from one of the motorcycle's leather bags. While one soldier held Sulka down, the other rubbed a liquid from the bottle on her lips. They forced her to drink water out of a canteen. She began to scream in pain. She died, screaming for me. Me. I couldn't rush out of hiding. I couldn't save her. I couldn't hug her. I dream about it."

✢ ✢ ✢

Freddie was dead wrong about finding a needle in the haystack. A glint of polished steel flashed up at the Thursday late show. A Swiss rare-stamp dealer was sitting in the audience at the cabaret. Just before noon the next morning, he turned up in the lobby of the Grand Hotel. Freddie came down in the elevator, and they took overstuffed chairs off the vast lobby.

"My name's Haim Galicia," he said. "Maybe your Nazi murderer was in my shop in Zurich. He was trying to sell me valuable stamps. He said he had an Inverted Jenny."

"A what, sir?"

"An American airmail stamp. Extremely rare, eh? Much sought after, yes? It shows an American airplane. A Jenny, it was called.

One sheet of stamps was printed upside down. So you have a great error. Only one hundred Inverted Jennies exist on the face of the earth. Can you imagine how expensive?"

"Very," replied Freddie.

"More than very."

"You bought it?"

"No," said the stamp dealer. "I assumed it was stolen. I could see from the numbers on the man's wrist that he was a concentration-camp survivor. The first letter, the J, told me at once he was a Jew. So I began talking to him in Yiddish. He didn't even seem to know 'nu' and 'shlemiel.' I smelled a rat. I suspected he was trying to sell stolen stamps. I said I'd need time to raise such a great amount of money if I chose to buy it. He said I'd better get busy, as he'd be leaving for New York in a few days, and he might sell it there."

Freddie paused briefly. "Did he smoke Egyptian cigarettes?"

"Yes. What Jew after the war could afford Egyptian cigarettes?"

Freddie's stomach tightened. Or was that the dybbuk doing handsprings? He'd found his man!

"He was an SS officer," said Freddie. "Do you know where he'll be staying in New York?"

"Me? No. But he won't be hard to find."

"Really?" Freddie thought the dybbuk must be holding his breath.

"Two months later, the stamp was sold in

New York, big news in our world. The buyer was well known. Look up Dr. Jameson T. Wixson in San Francisco, yes? I have seen in the press that he continues to buy rarities from the counterfeit Jew. He undoubtedly knows your man's whereabouts."

Freddie nodded, smiling. "Leave your card, sir. I'll make sure you receive a reward."

"*Feh,*" he said, a grin on his lips. "I'm not tempted by your reward. Give it to a Jewish charity, eh?"

Within an hour, Freddie had posted a cable to the doctor in San Francisco. The following evening he received a cable in return. The German dealer in rare stamps was standing trial for murder in Phoenix, Arizona.

CHAPTER
⇒ 18 ⇐

When Freddie told his girlfriend that he had bought a ticket on the *Mauritania* to New York, her face blossomed into a sunflower smile. "You darling man, we can have the captain marry us!"

Freddie averted his eyes. How could he face her? "Polly, I love you like in that Portuguese sonnet, but we can't get hitched yet."

"Freddie, what kind of a stall is this?"

How do you break the news that you are possessed? She'd be marrying the dybbuk without knowing it. When she found out, live steam would shoot out of her ears.

"I should be back in a month or so."

"Why can't we marry now?"

"Trust me."

There was no mistaking Polly's look of distress. "Freddie, I think you're a dog that won't hunt! Another woman? Here's your ring back."

"No other woman. I didn't give you a ring."

"Well, if you had, here it is back!" And, lifting her chin like the prow of a ship, Polly sailed away.

Freddie watched her go and spiraled down into a funk. He stood on a trafficky corner, unsure which way to turn. A wind off the river blew his hair about like a head of snakes. Taxi horns blew him across the street. What should he do?

He loved Polly. She needed to know about the dybbuk. He must tell her before he left. Okay. He'd risk it. He'd do it.

For ten days Freddie was unable to reach her by phone. She was even avoiding their restaurants and cafés. She seemed to have vanished in an angry puff of smoke. Had she slipped out of town? Not even her friends had a clue.

Packing for the trip, he said in mournful

tones, "Dybbuk! See what a mess you're making of my life? Why am I going to New York for you? What a sap I am!"

"You wouldn't let me down," said the dybbuk.

"Why not?"

"Because you're a mensch."

"Don't give me that Jewish stuff. I can get along without you in the act."

"Almost, yes. Have you looked in a mirror lately, Professor? I see you are now talking without moving the lips."

CHAPTER

❈ 19 ❈

The steamship picked up its last passengers in Ireland and set out across the Atlantic Ocean. A sea wind was blowing up whitecaps like dollops of meringue. It was going to be a choppy crossing.

The third day, just before Freddie left his cabin for breakfast, the dybbuk spoke up. "Please, Professor, no bacon with your eggs this morning. Ask for the kosher meals."

Freddie's mouth dropped. "Kosher. No!"

"Do us a favor and eat kosher, yes."

Freddie pulled open the stateroom door. "Us?"

"I'm feeling a little seasick."

Freddie let his breath whistle out. How was someone possessed by a demon supposed to live? Like a prisoner? But what was he going to do if he discovered a seasick dybbuk under his skin? The thought almost turned him green. "Okay, Avrom Amos. Kosher for a couple of days, until we land. Boy, it's not easy to be a Jew."

"You just finding out?" remarked the dybbuk. "Did I tell you what I used to carry in my pocket?"

"A kosher slingshot?"

"A bottle of carbolic acid."

"Nothing about you surprises me."

"I was hiding from the Nazis, eleven years old. When I heard them getting close I'd sprinkle carbolic on my sister's clothes and mine. We'd curl up like dead. *Oh*, how we stunk of sickness! We'd hear the SS killers yell warnings. 'Typhus! Don't touch them!' Until the bottle ran dry, the carbolic saved our lives. Yes, it's hard to be one of the chosen people. Did we volunteer? Did the Almighty ask for a show of hands?"

Freddie had blintzes for breakfast.

❖ ❖ ❖

Of course it was Polly. That showgirl with her hair cut gamine short. That figure in the deck chair wrapped in a blanket against the cold. She had followed him and now was busy hiding her face behind a book.

Freddie barked in astonishment. "Polly! Sweetheart! How did you get here?"

She lowered the book. "Do I know you?"

"I've got to talk to you, Polly."

"Some other time. I'm going home for a visit. There are people there who love me."

"I adore you!" Freddie declared. "I've missed you. I don't want to lose you. I'll tell you everything. But hang on to your hat."

"Tell me what? You've got a wife in Toledo?"

"Worse."

"Your doctor has given you only twenty minutes to live?"

"Much worse." Freddie pushed aside her feet and sat on the edge of the lounge chair. "I've been possessed."

He waited for a reaction. She turned a page of her book. "Imagine."

"You're not taking this very seriously," he protested. "I'm possessed by a demon. It's not just part of my act."

"Oh, come on," Polly said.

"A Jewish demon. A dybbuk. I tried to have it exorcised, but it didn't take."

"Did you try Epsom salts?"

"Polly, please."

She put down her book. "Freddie, this is not the dark ages. Someone turned on the lights. Who believes in that possessed-by-demon stuff anymore? I don't."

"I don't either. Didn't. But the dybbuk is here. So I couldn't let you marry me. Understand?"

"Freddie, have you talked to a psychiatrist?"

"You can talk to him yourself."

"A psychiatrist?"

"The dybbuk. Avrom Amos Poliakov, meet Polly Marchant. Polly, meet the dybbuk. He's just a kid, but he's older'n

God. He'll tell you so himself."

Polly peered at Freddie. "Do you take me for a nitwit?"

Freddie felt the breath rise through his throat. "Good afternoon," said the dybbuk. Very civil.

Polly's breath caught. Then she exhaled like a steam whistle. "You just threw your voice. That's what you do. You're a ventriloquist. You threw your voice!"

"I swear I didn't!"

"I swear he didn't, too," said the dybbuk. "It's me, in person."

"Listen, Polly," Freddie exclaimed. "Avrom and I can sing a duet. That'll prove there are two of us!"

"Do you know 'Yankee Doodle'?" asked the dybbuk.

"Go."

The Great Freddie and the dybbuk broke into a few bars in harmony. Polly gazed into Freddie's mouth, past his teeth, and down his throat as far as she could see. Yes, there was another voice down there. She was far from cheered by the discovery.

"You expect me to marry a guy with a demon down his gullet?"

"I'm not a demon," protested the dybbuk.

Polly dropped the book and folded her arms. "Cough him up or leave me alone, Freddie."

"It's not that simple. Just give me a couple

more weeks to straighten this thing out, Polly darling. Things are happening and I made promises."

"You made promises to me! Remember? I'm not going to go on my honeymoon with you and that spooky tapeworm. Out, spirit! Out, ghostie, and right now!"

"Polly—"

"Don't ask me to be patient!"

"Be patient. You're getting excited about nothing."

Polly exploded. "Nothing!"

"Give me a week," Freddie said.

"How about five minutes?" Her eyes began to tear. "If you loved me—"

Freddie straightened and waited. Then he

turned his head as if the dybbuk were hovering at his left. "Avrom Amos, you heard Polly. You know about love, don't you? I promised to hang in for you, but love is trump. No messing with that. You were listening to every word, huh? Polly didn't mean that bit about the tapeworm. But the time has come. Five minutes. Pack your socks and sweater, kid. It was a great bother knowing you, but no hard feelings. Now take a walk and good luck!"

It was a moment before the dybbuk answered. "The Great Freddie, be kind enough to look over the rail. What do you see? Oy, you expect me to walk on water?"

"It's been done."

"I can't even swim."

"So long, Avrom Amos."

"And what would you do for a stage act?"

"I'll work up some new tricks."

"Do you think I like being under your skin? It's crowded in here. And do you think it's fun for me when you lift weights?"

"Dybbuk, see the tears in Polly's eyes? We want to get married. Be a mensch. Get lost."

"If you have a wedding, count on me. You won't know I'm there. Until then, if you don't mind, I'll curl up for a long nap. I'll need all my strength for Arizona."

And the dybbuk clammed up, silent as a mouse, until the ship docked in New York. Polly felt triumphant.

CHAPTER

❖ 20 ❖

Polly's family had driven up from Alabama to greet Polly as she stepped off the ship. They threw handfuls of confetti as if it were rice.

Polly disentangled herself from relatives and turned to Freddie. "This is my mother, Belle Marchant, and my two younger sisters, Twayla and Eva." All three women wore big floppy hats and summer dresses. They looked fetching, Freddie thought, but were wet as goldfish. It was late August and full of lightning and warm rain.

"Charmed to meet you, dear boy," said Mrs. Marchant, anointing him with damp confetti as freely as holy water. "Polly wrote that you're Jewish. We'll be the scandal of Mobile."

Freddie gave an inward sigh. Wait till they learned about the dybbuk.

Polly indicated a man chewing tobacco in a dark suit and tight vest and a gray Stetson hat. "And this is my horrible uncle Wimble. He's the family racist. I'm sure he's never shaken hands with a Jewish man before. Do assure him it's not catching."

Uncle Wimble kept his hands stuck in his pockets as if by glue. It surprised Freddie that he felt so offended. For Avrom's sake, or his own? At any rate, he couldn't resist the moment. As they were walking away from the ship, The Great Freddie threw his voice, angrily, to a nearby trash bin. "The Hebrews are coming! It's payback time, brothers! Run for your lives."

Uncle Wimble jerked around as if struck by a bolt of lightning. He swallowed a mouthful of chewing tobacco.

Mrs. Marchant cut in smartly with a nod to Polly. "Have you two darlings set a date?"

"Of course," said Polly. "As soon as possible."

"Good. That leaves us plenty of time to make the arrangements."

After a shopping day in New York, Freddie confessed to Polly that the dybbuk hadn't really fled, but soon would. Positively. Absolutely. Honestly. Truly. I promise. I swear. On my honor!

Leaving her in tears, Freddie hopped a train out west. He settled back for a three-day trip. It was only after the delay in Chicago to change trains that the dybbuk chose to speak up. "Are we there yet?"

"I need to talk to you."

"Shoot."

"You're overstaying your welcome."

"What's a day or two?"

"It's been months!" Freddie exclaimed. "Here are the new house rules. I'll see you through Phoenix, but that's where you get off. We split. If not, I'll make your time in my skin miserable."

"You think it's a picnic?" asked the dybbuk.

"I'll gorge like a pig on trayf!" Freddie had already learned the Yiddish word for pork and shellfish and other forbidden food. "I'll move to Mobile and retire the act. And I'll join the Ku Klux Klan!"

"Oy gevalt!"

"No options. No loopholes. That's the deal. Got it?"

"We'll see," remarked the dybbuk, and went back to sleep.

In Phoenix, Freddie checked into the Biltmore Hotel. He began telephoning Polly in Mobile every day, and every day she refused to come to the phone. But he was confident she'd soften when he could tell her the dybbuk had fled.

He bought a newspaper moments after checking into the hotel. Once in his room overlooking desert and cactus, he found the news he was hoping for. "Wake up, Avrom Amos," he said, folding his newspaper.

"Listen to this. Your SS man is charged with killing a young assistant in his stamp business. He thought the employee was stealing from him—and get this. The assistant was a mere kid of fifteen. Right in character, for a child killer."

The dybbuk remained profoundly silent. It seemed to Freddie that, now that they were so close to Avrom Amos's murderer, the dybbuk had frozen up. Unsure of himself. By dinnertime, Freddie began to wonder if the dybbuk had bailed out. There seemed to be nobody in.

Had the dybbuk lost his grit? How, after all, could he hope to achieve his biblical revenge? Freddie wasn't going to pick up a knife or a gun and do some murderous deed.

No, the dybbuk had something else less lethal but more mortifying up his sleeve. He'd tipped his hand after his bar mitzvah.

The trial resumed at ten the following morning. Freddie came early and commandeered a freshly polished oak chair in the second row. The courtroom filled rapidly and heated up. The wooden blades of a ceiling fan stirred the desert air in slow motion. A couple of newspapermen arrived at the last moment, seating themselves at a desk for the press.

The bailiff introduced the Honorable Harold O. Fanshaw, judge of the Superior Court, who settled himself in his black robe like a thundercloud. He banged his gavel and the courtroom went silent. "Open for business," the judge declared. "Where's the defendant?"

The defendant arrived moments later. He took the witness stand, all but clicking his heels. Freddie gave the former SS officer's face a hard, piercing gaze. So this was the face of a killer. This was the man who had shown such enthusiasm for child murder? The former German officer who had shot Avrom Amos six times?

The German was no longer wearing his vulture black uniform with its death's-head insignia. He was no longer smoking Egyptian cigarettes, but the dueling scars and hatchet-sharp nose still had their arrogant presence.

The defense attorney rose to continue his case. A portly man, he pulled off his horn-rimmed glasses and threw them angrily on the table.

"So what do you see? A kindly old refugee with numbers tattooed on his wrist. J for Jew. A survivor of the Nazi death factories. Years pass. An unfortunate child chooses to take poison. And my client is charged with murder? Preposterous! What motive? May I remind you that poison residue was detected on the young man's lips? Does that sound like murder? The rat poison was self-administered. That is clear! Suicide, open and shut, shut, shut."

Freddie looked around as if he might spot the dybbuk hiding among the spectators.

The defense attorney blew hot and hotter until the judge banged his gavel and ordered a break for lunch. But not before the attorney announced defiantly that he would put his client on the witness stand to remove all doubt of any guilt.

Freddie wasn't hungry and wandered outside to find a stone bench and sit in the desert sun. It was then that the dybbuk seemed to shake off his sullen lethargy and come to life.

"Thank you, Mr. Freddie. Thank you, Mr. Yankee Doodle. You were a good Jew when I needed you."

"What are you talking about? Where have you been?"

"This is when we shake hands. Now we go our separate ways."

"You're leaving just when you have the

monster in your sights? Isn't it him? Wrong
SS officer?"

"It's him."

"And you're backing out?"

"You're free of me. That's what I'm trying
to tell you."

"I'm no longer possessed?"

"So long, Mr. Yankel Doodle," said the
dybbuk. "Don't forget to pay the charity for
the Swiss stamp dealer."

"Of course. What are you going to do?"

"Don't ask questions."

"What am I going to do?" asked Freddie.

"You can work up an act without moving
your lips. A showstopper!"

Me, work solo? Me, The Great Freddie?

He could see nothing but disaster waiting in the wings. He was going to have to walk out into the spotlight practically naked. The dybbuk wasn't going to be there with his sharp tongue to make The Great Freddie sound like a top attraction.

The act was finished. His young partner would vanish. Turn to smoke. Be forever gone.

The entertainer straightened his shoulders. Freddie, he thought, you're hopeless. Can't you even talk to yourself without moving your lips? Did you ever once stop to realize how much you'll miss that war-wounded kid? Remember when he was your only real knockabout friend? Ingrate! Did it ever occur to you to say thanks?

"Thanks. I'll miss you, Avrom Amos."

"Like a toothache, eh? It's been a pleasure, Mr. Freddie T. Birch. So, now you are free to rush back and marry that girl," said the dybbuk. "Mazel tov! Maybe I'll find a way to send a wedding gift."

"I'll take it out of your salary," said Freddie, trying to soften the moment with a green-eyed smile. "I guess I won't see you again—ever?"

"L'chaim," said the dybbuk. "To life, eh? I'll put in a good word for you if you decide to visit our heaven. You are a righteous mensch. The door'll be wide open. Break a leg."

"Not so fast!" Freddie protested. "Avrom Amos, hold on! What's the big rush?"

But the dybbuk was gone.

CHAPTER

✦ 21 ✦

The former SS officer took the witness stand as if it were a fortress to be defended. The desert sun now shot through the single window and threw a white hot spotlight on him. The defendant snapped up his right hand, eager to take the oath again. He stood under the ceiling fan, straight and almost tall enough for the blades to crop his yellow hair.

The defense lawyer fixed a fist on his hip. "Tell us, sir, in your own words, how you found the body."

"Dead," replied the German, with a sharp shrug. "Dead, and holding his stomach. What a stupid boy, eh? I knew he was stealing stamps. Trash stamps. I was glad to be rid of them, yes? Not even my worst enemy thinks I would poison the boy over a pocketful of wastepaper."

"You have enemies, Mr. Goldstein?" asked the attorney.

"Not a single one in the whole world. *Nein. Non.*"

"Why would the boy take poison and commit suicide?"

"You ask me? All I know, he chose my backyard to die. Rat poison. An accident, eh?"

The attorney hoisted a confident smile. "So you are innocent?"

Before the defendant could answer, he gave a sort of hiccup and out came *"Heil Hitler!"*

Involuntarily, his right arm rose in the beginning of a stiff-armed Nazi salute. Regaining his composure, the former officer clapped his arm back to his side.

It was clear that he was stunned. Where had that voice come from?

Freddie was the only person in the courtroom whose face burst into a smile. He knew where the voice had come from! He knew what the cunning Avrom Amos was up to. The dybbuk was possessing SS Officer Gerhard Junker-Strupp!

The judge said, "You are declaring your confounded innocence?"

"Certainly!" cried out the German.

"—*Not*," added the dybbuk. *"Certainly not!"*

The courtroom seemed to catch its breath. The defendant went pale. His jaw fell open. He was struck dumb. He couldn't grasp what was happening to his voice; he tried to clear it.

"Are you pleading guilty?" asked the judge, astonished.

Again, the dybbuk's voice came blustering out. "Do I look innocent? Guilty, a hundred percent!"

"I object!" cried out the defense attorney. "My client declares his innocence!"

"Let him declare for himself," said the judge.

The former officer tried to pull himself together, but he seemed frozen by panic, and the dybbuk overrode his voice.

"What kind of a donkey trial is this, eh? I said I was guilty. I hired my lawyer to lie for me. *Achtung!* Here is some truth. My name is not Goldstein. I had those Auschwitz numbers tattooed on my wrist to fool you. I am Colonel Gerhard Junker-Strupp, *hauptschar-führer-SS* of the proud death heads of Germany! *Heil Hitler!*"

"I object, I object," the defense attorney

bellowed. "The defendant is suddenly talking nonsense!"

"You object?" said the dybbuk. "I object. I am under oath. You are not. Sit down."

"Well put," remarked the judge. "Continue, Mr. Goldstein."

"Junker-Strupp, sir. My stamp assistant was murdered! You want an eyewitness? You are looking at an eyewitness. Me! You want experience? I had orders to hunt down Jewkids and wipe them off the face of the earth. We used to pull that same poisoning trick in Germany. Why waste a bullet on the non-Aryan garbage? I confess I poisoned my stamp assistant!"

By this time, the former officer was

jerking around as if pulled by strings. He covered his mouth with his arm, but still words came tripping forth. His eyes rolled in a surging panic.

Freddie sat back, folded his arms, and enjoyed the show. How adroit the dybbuk was! And what a hopeless fool the mass murderer appeared to be, now trying to stuff his mouth with a clenched fist. Bravo, Avrom Amos! Out through the German's ram's horn of a nose came his confession. "So, jury! So, Judge! What was my motive? What else? The boy discovered papers. He learned who I really am, a war criminal with a noose waiting for me. Why else would I kill the boy? Why else?"

"Is that your sworn testimony?" asked the judge, hunching forward.

The defendant pulled his knuckles free of his mouth to protest, but the dybbuk drowned him out. "I'm guilty! You, at the typing machine—are you getting this down? I, Colonel Gerhard Junker-Strupp, former SS officer, I poisoned the boy! In my native Germany, I directed the murder of whole trainloads of children. Some by my own hand. I remember a redheaded kid, Avrom Amos Poliakov by name. I shot him. His sister, Sulka. She, we poisoned. For those petty crimes alone, I should have your death penalty twice over! For the other little Jews, a million times over! Guilty! Guilty, jury, from

top to bottom! I'm late for my own hanging.
So kindly hurry it up, Judge."

As if struck by lightning, the newspapermen went flying to telephones to get this
bombshell of a story in print. The judge sat
back. He seemed to enjoy the chaos in his
courtroom as a refreshment from dreary
shoplifting and burglary trials.

The SS officer collapsed in his chair, a
gaze of profound confusion and vagueness in
his eyes. Had he suddenly gone mad? Who
had known these darkest war secrets of his?

Freddie gazed at him and could see his
future more clearly than any crystal ball could
reveal. Until his last day on earth, the
German was going to be possessed by a

Jewish dybbuk. Avrom Amos was going to drive him crazy.

Freddie sent a flick of a wave toward the witness stand. He felt sure the dybbuk was looking at him.

"Mazel tov, pal," Freddie said. "L'chaim!"

He didn't move his lips.

✤ Author's Note ✤

Who could have imagined that the witch's oven in Hansel and Gretel would leap out of the storybooks and into real life? It happened in Germany, during the 1930s and 1940s.

Jewish children by the cattle carloads were delivered to the gas ovens and death factories during World War II. Why the hunt for children? Among Nazi calculations at the highest level was a fear that the Jewish young, if allowed to grow up, would seek revenge for the slaughter of their parents. No Jewish child was to be left breathing. Europe was to become *Judenfrie*—free of Jews.

Before being crushed and surrendering in 1945, the Nazis came close to succeeding. The human butchery and smoking crematoria were unprecedented in history. The events have come to be known as the Holocaust. The word is from the Greek, meaning to be burned whole.

For a few coins, bounty hunters searched out children in hiding and delivered them to the Nazis. There were special days set aside to rid the cities and villages of Jewish kids, as in this story. Collecting the terrified young in sacks, like stray cats, really happened, too. And yes, painting childish lips with poisons happened. Poison was cheaper than bullets, and what was a mere Jewish child worth?

It is surprising how many fragmentary diaries kept by children of the Holocaust have survived and been published. Here and there, I have slipped into this narrative a few trembling words still fresh from the tragic past.

It has taken me a long lifetime of novel writing to finally feel prepared to grapple with the Holocaust. But what tale to tell? There was a horror story in every victim. At the same time, the indomitable Jewish sense of humor somehow survived.

It was only when I began wondering about a dybbuk, the ghost of a murdered child, perhaps, that I found a spotlight to shine on the nightmare of the centuries. Could I allow in the occasional shaft of sunlight—the tough Jewish sense of humor?

History is easy to forget. Does it matter in our contemporary lives if we toss aside what happened so long ago? If we forget—*poof!*—history vanishes. The Holocaust vanishes. If we don't know where we have been, how wise will we be in the future?

I remember as a child of eight being told by a young friend that I had killed Christ.

That was news to me. It's a common experience for the Jewish young. Should later generations of Germans be burdened with the guilt arising from the profound inhumanity of their ancestors? Revenge may be sweet, but guilt is nontransferable. Still, hatreds survive with the persistence of cockroaches.

Do I believe in dybbuks, misty ghosts, imps, and other ancient and fabled creatures? Only if it turns out that the earth is, indeed, flat.

L'chaim!

—Sid Fleischman
Santa Monica, California